Stories of
GIANTS

Christopher Rawson
Adapted by Gill Harvey

Illustrated by
Stephen Cartwright

Reading Consultant: Alison Kelly
University of Surrey Roehampton

D1365014

Contents

Chapter 1

All kinds of giants

There are lots of stories about giants – and lots of different giants. Some were quite small, but most were **enormous**!

There were naughty ones...

...wild ones, who liked nothing better than to fight...

...sad ones, who never stopped crying...

...and kind ones, who helped grannies.

The first story is about a good giant called a troll. The second tells of three wicked giants and how they met a grisly end.

Chapter 2

Jon and the green troll

Once, there was a poor farmer. His wife was dead. He lived with his only son, Jon, by the mountains in Scotland.

In the spring and summer,
Jon and his father worked
hard in the fields.

In the autumn, they closed
the farm and went down to
the sea, to fish.

But, one year, Jon's father felt too old for the trip.

"You'll have to go alone," he said to Jon.

"Just remember one thing," he warned. "Don't stop at the big, black rock. That's where the trolls live."

As Jon drove up a rocky mountain path, the sky grew dark. Then a storm blew up. Lightning flashed and thunder growled. Jon wanted his dad.

At last, he saw a big, black rock. "Ah! I can shelter there," he thought.

Jon had forgotten his father's warning. He was just glad to be out of the storm. He sat down outside a cave.

"Time for supper," he said to himself, and unpacked his sack. He had bread, cheese, an apple and a very big fish.

Mmm... Crusty bread and smelly cheese. Delicious!

Suddenly, Jon heard a
noise coming from inside
the cave. He was so scared,
he stopped chewing.

Wha...
what's that?

He could hear voices –
babies' voices! "Wahhh!"
they cried. "We're hungry!"

Jon quickly picked up the fish and cut it in half. He threw both halves into the cave.

The crying stopped at once.

"Whew," said Jon. "Thank goodness for that."

13

He was almost asleep when a giant shadow fell over him. Jon looked up. A troll! A troll was coming for him...

Now, he remembered his father's warning. But it was too late.

The troll came over to Jon and picked him up. He shook with terror. This was his first fishing trip alone – and he was the one to be caught.

Please don't eat me!

But the troll was gentle. "Don't be scared," she said. "I want to thank you for feeding my children."

The troll took Jon into her cave and looked after him. She even gave him her children's bed. It was lumpy but Jon slept well.

Who's sleeping in my bed?

The next morning, after breakfast, the troll waved Jon off.

"Take these magic fishing hooks," she said. "When you reach the sea, look for an old man called Charlie. You must go fishing with him."

Only fish near the pointed rock.

"Thank you," said Jon.
"I will."

Jon did just as the troll had said. He found Charlie in an old hut by the beach.

"Will you come fishing with me?" asked Jon.

Why me?

"Are you sure?" said Charlie. "I'm the worst fisherman in the world. I never catch anything."

Charlie showed Jon his boat. It was full of holes and falling to pieces.

"Don't worry!" said Jon. "I can soon fix that."

He set to work with some tar

and planks of wood. Soon, the boat was as good as new.

"Let's row to that pointed rock," Jon said to Charlie. They put worms on the magic hooks, and started to fish.

"Hey!" Jon cried, a few seconds later. "I've caught one!"

"So have I!" shouted Charlie.

They couldn't believe their luck. The boat was full of fish!

The other fishermen couldn't believe it either.

Jon told them to fish near the pointed rock. But when they tried, they didn't catch a thing.

Every day for the entire
winter, Jon's magic hooks
caught hundreds of fish.

Every day, Jon and Charlie cleaned the fish and hung them up to dry. They had more fish than all the other fishermen put together.

When spring came, it was time for Jon to go home. On the way, he visited the troll and gave her half his fish.

"Thank you," she said. "One day, you'll have a dream about me. When you do, you must come back to my cave."

Back at home, Jon helped his father on the farm. A year later, he had a dream about the troll – just as she had said.

He quickly left for her cave, without telling his father where he was going.

At last, he reached the cave.
He peered inside.

"Hello?"
he called.
"Is anybody
home?"
There was
no answer.

Jon crept into the cave. It
was empty except for
two chests.

"Are they
for me?" Jon
wondered.
What could
be inside?

He put the chests on his cart and took them home. When he opened them, he found piles of treasure and gold. Jon and his father were so rich, they never had to work again.

Chapter 3

The princess and the giants

On the edge of a gloomy wood, three giants were eating their dinner.

28

These giants were gigantic. They were eating meat as big as rocks. Their spoons were like shovels and their forks were big enough to dig a garden.

But someone was secretly watching them.

His name was Sam and he was a hunter.

"I'm going to have some fun with these giants," he said.

Taking aim, he fired his gun at the fork of the fattest giant.

Sam's gun made the giant jump. He poked the fork into his chin.

"Ow!" he yelled. "Who did that?"

Sam tried to hide, but he wasn't quick enough. The giant spotted him.

He jumped up and grabbed Sam. "Ha ha! Now you're in trouble, boy!" he roared.

"Unless you help us," he added. "We want the princess from the king's castle. You can get her."

"H-how?" squeaked Sam.
He was terrified.

"Oh, we'll show you," the
giant said. He laughed.

The giants picked up Sam and took him to the castle.

"Everyone's asleep," they told him. "We put a spell on them. But the dog is still awake. You must shoot him."

They pushed Sam through a tiny window.

The castle dog trotted up to Sam, wagging his tail. He didn't bark once. He was a very friendly dog.

Hello there! What's your name?

"How could I shoot you?" asked Sam, patting him.

Sam decided he wasn't going to help the giants. "I think I'll explore the castle," he said.

In one room, Sam found the princess. He thought she was beautiful. He gazed at her for a long, long time. Then he tiptoed out.

Next, he found a room with a sword hanging on the wall. There was a golden cup beside the sword, with writing on it.

Drink this and you will save the princess with the magic sword, read Sam.

Sam was excited. Perhaps he could save the princess from those horrible giants. He tried a sip of the drink...

He drank some more. Soon, he'd finished it.

"Now for the sword!" said Sam. He gave a big tug and felt it move, just a little. He tried again.

Got it!

This time, it came out in a rush. "Ha ha!" said Sam. "Now to get those giants!"

Downstairs, the giants were knocking at the door.

"Let us in!" they bellowed.

"You're too big and the door's too small," said Sam.

"Never mind that!" yelled the giants. "Open this door now!"

"OK," said Sam and he hid behind the door...

As the giants crawled in, he chopped off their heads. The princess was saved.

But Sam began to worry. The king might not like people using his sword. He could be in big trouble. So he ran away.

Back in the castle, the giants' spell soon wore off. The soldiers woke up. They stared at the dead giants. Could it really be true?

The king! The king! Fetch the king!

Someone's killed the giants!

The castle buzzed with excitement. The giants were dead at last. But who had killed them?

The king saw that his sword had gone, too. It was a mystery.

The princess was happiest of all. She dreamed of the handsome hero who had saved her.

"Please find him for me, Daddy," she begged.

So the king built an inn. A sign above the door

read: *Anyone who tells his life story may stay here for free.*

A year later, Sam passed by. He went inside and told his tale.

It's the giant killer! Call the princess!

The king was overjoyed to meet the man who'd killed the giants. His daughter was so excited, she married Sam that very day.

Everyone was invited to the wedding... except giants. None of the other giants would have gone anyway. They were far too scared of Sam.

Try these other books in
Series One:

The Burglar's Breakfast: Alfie
Briggs is a burglar. After a hard
night of thieving, he likes to go home
to a tasty meal. But one day he gets
back to discover someone has
stolen his breakfast!

The Dinosaurs Next Door: Stan
loves living next door to Mr. Puff.
His house is full of amazing things.
Best of all are the dinosaur eggs –
until they begin to hatch...

The Monster Gang: Starting a
gang is a great idea. So is dressing
up like monsters. But if everyone
is in disguise, how do you know
who's who?

Series editor: Lesley Sims

Designed by
Katarina Dragoslavić

This edition first published in 2002 by Usborne Publishing Ltd.,
Usborne House, 83-85 Saffron Hill, London EC1N 8RT, England.
www.usborne.com
Copyright © 2002, 1980 Usborne Publishing Ltd.